10e

10855833

This Ladybird book

belongs to

_____

Published by Ladybird Books Ltd
80 Strand London WC2R 0RL
A Penguin Company
9 10 8

Printed in Italy

Beep! Beep!
first picture
word book

illustrated by Angie Sage

house

shop

Barp! Barp!

bus

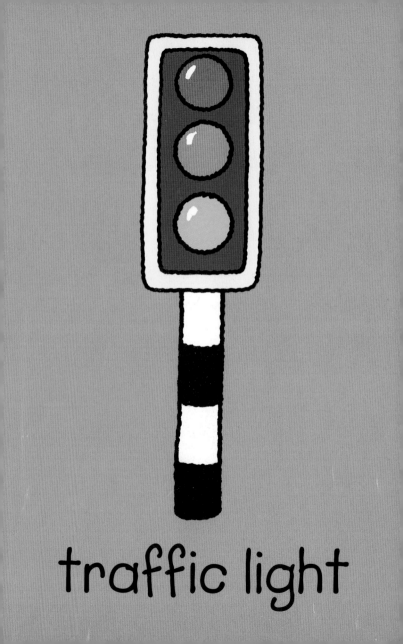

traffic light

train

Vroo-oom!

plane

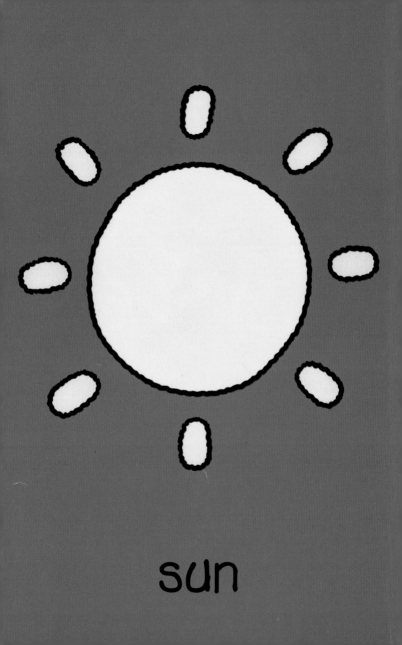

sun

rain

bicycle

Brrm! Brrm!

digger

garage

supermarket

moon

stars

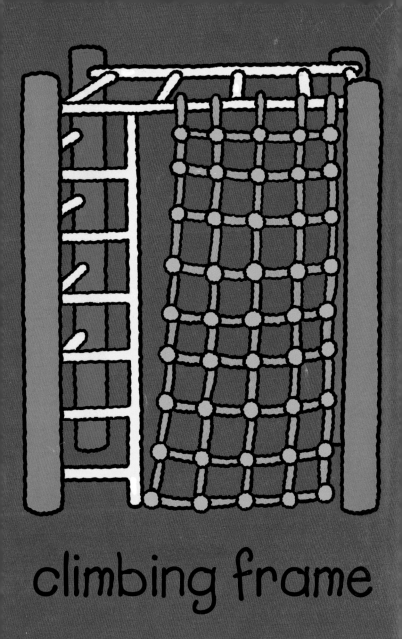

climbing frame

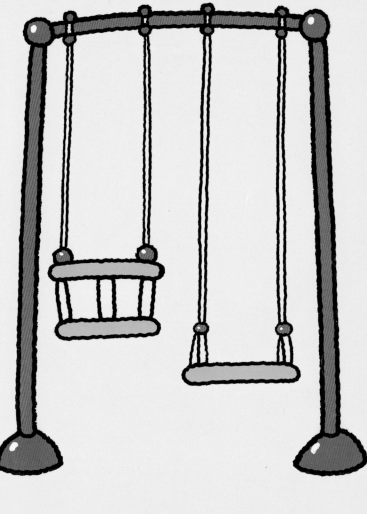

swings

Splash! Splosh!

paddling pool

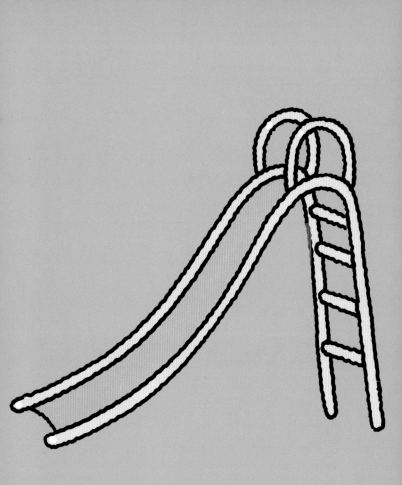

slide

Chug! Chug!

tractor

Baa! Baa!

sheep